THIS BOOK BELONGS TO

....

Billie's Vacation

····· WRITTEN BY ·····
Michael Kennedy

····· ILLUSTRATED BY ·····
Jean Tower

Illustrations by Jean Tower
Book design by The Troy Book Makers

Printed in the United States of America

The Troy Book Makers • Troy, New York • thetroybookmakers.com

To order additional copies of this title, contact your favorite local bookstore or visit www.shoptbmbooks.com

ISBN: 978-1-61468-484-8

DEDICATED TO

The Kenbright Grandchildren:
Wesley, Cecelia, Ada, Cora (and one more on the way).

The CADASIL Community

Billie M.

. . . .

SPECIAL THANKS TO

Jean T.

Allison M.

Jim L.

. . . .

IN MEMORY OF

Barbara Kennedy

Jojo, Madison Blues and Rocco

ABOUT CADASIL AND CURECADASIL.ORG

· ·

cureCADASIL.org is a nonprofit organization that started with a handful of dedicated volunteers in 2012 as CADASIL Association. These people saw a need for a group to work toward a cure for this serious neurological disease. Since that time, we have been fortunate to make great strides in our mission to raise awareness of CADASIL, ensuring it will be universally recognized and understood by the medical community, enabling patients to be correctly diagnosed. We are dedicated to helping all touched by CADASIL, improving education available on CADASIL and promote and support research for this rare disease.

CADASIL stands for Cerebral Autosomal Dominant Arteriopathy with Subcortical Infarcts and Leukoencephalopathy. It is a Notch 3 genetic degenerative neurological disease that effects the brain and other areas of the body. Symptoms of CADASIL include migraine with aura, strokes, mood disorders, fatigue, ischemic episodes/TIAs, visual disturbances, cognitive issues, seizures, and dementia. Symptoms vary between patients, even those within the same family. CADASIL can be misdiagnosed as MS/Multiple Sclerosis and other neurological conditions.

CADASIL is typically diagnosed in adulthood, but as awareness of the disease grows, some patients have been diagnosed in childhood, and more people are being correctly diagnosed. We are grateful for the medical professionals conducting research in various parts of the world to cure CADASIL and are hopeful for a breakthrough.

CADASIL runs in families and can effect everyone in a family regardless of whether every member carries the gene for it or not. There are a number of support groups on Facebook for patients, families, and friends, as being able to talk to others who understand is vitally important.

**For more information about CADASIL,
please go to: cureCADASIL.org**

info@ cureCADASIL.org

BILLIE'S MOMMY AND DADDY WERE GOING ON A CRUISE.

WHILE THEY WERE PACKING, POOR BILLIE CAME DOWN WITH THE BLUES.

BILLIE COULD NOT STAY AT HOME ALL ALONE —

WHO WOULD FEED HIM? WHO WOULD GIVE HIM A BONE?

WHO WOULD WALK HIM EACH MORNING? AND AGAIN AT NIGHT?

WHO WOULD THROW HIS TOYS, SO THEY WOULD BOUNCE JUST RIGHT?

BILLIE WAS WORRIED AND A BIT OUT OF SORT —

HE'D NEVER BEEN TO A PUPPY RESORT!

JUST DOWN THE ROAD,
NOT MORE THAN A MILE,

WHEN BILLIE SAW THE RESORT,
HE BEGAN TO SMILE!

HIS ROOM HAD A BIG BED; HE COULD SLEEP; HE COULD NAP.

AND SOME OF THE HELPERS LET BILLIE REST ON THEIR LAP.

EVERY MORNING, A HELPER SAT NEAR BILLIE'S FEET —

DRINKING HIS COFFEE WHILE BILLIE WOULD EAT!

BILLIE WAGGED HIS TAIL WITH EVERY BITE AND NIBBLE.

HE ATE EVERY LAST DROP OF HIS CHICKEN AND KIBBLE.

WHEN BREAKFAST WAS DONE,
BILLIE JUMPED ON HIS BED —

WHERE A HELPER SAT
AND RUBBED BILLIE'S HEAD.

BILLIE LICKED THE HELPER,
THEN HOPPED TO THE FLOOR,

AND FOLLOWED HIS NEW FRIEND
OUT THROUGH THE DOOR.

PAST A ROOM ON THE LEFT AND A ROOM ON THE RIGHT.

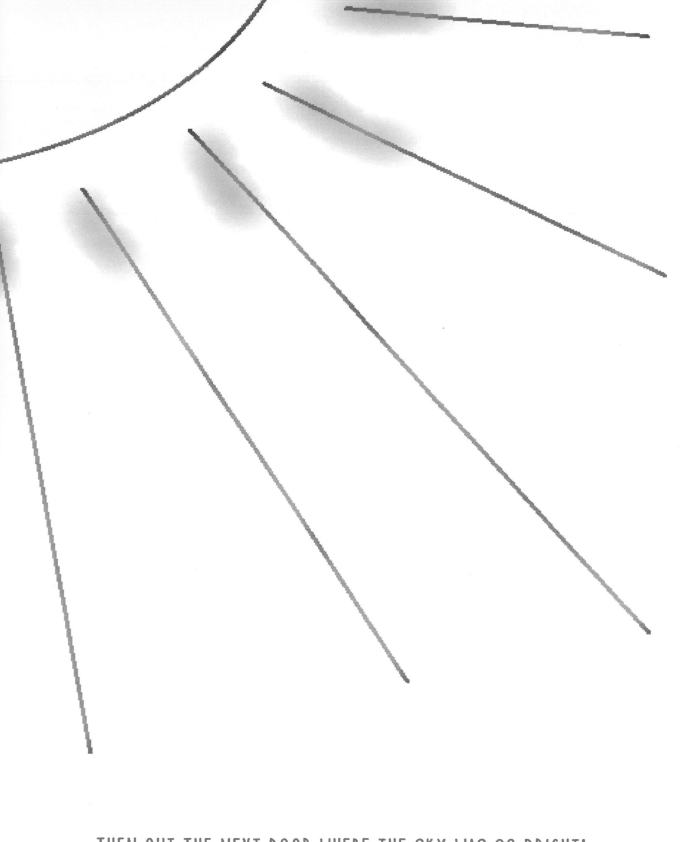

THEN OUT THE NEXT DOOR WHERE THE SKY WAS SO BRIGHT!

OUTSIDE HE WENT, TO THE WARM, MORNING SUN,

TO A REALLY BIG YARD, TO JUMP AND TO RUN.

OTHER PUPPIES WERE THERE, TO WRESTLE AND CHASE —

TO SEE WHO WOULD WIN RACE AFTER RACE.

THAT NIGHT, BILLIE LAID HIS HEAD DOWN TO REST -

THINKING...

"OH, WOW! TODAY WAS THE BEST!"

FOR FIVE MORE DAYS, BILLIE WOULD PLAY —
EACH MORNING AN ADVENTURE, ANOTHER GREAT DAY!

WHEN MOMMY AND DADDY CAME BACK, BILLIE WAS GLAD —

HE BARKED, AND HE WIGGLED TO SHOW THE FUN THAT HE HAD!

BILLIE LOVED THE RESORT AND ENJOYED HIS STAY.

HE HAD MADE NEW FRIENDS WHO COULD RUN, WHO COULD PLAY!

BUT HE HAD A FAVORITE PLACE,
TO RUN AND TO ROAM.

HE JUMPED IN HIS CAR:
HE WAS READY FOR HOME!